Old Moo

MW01234184

Volume IV

Published by Old Moon Quarterly.

Each author retains the copyright to their story.

This is a work of fiction. Names, characters, places and incidents either are the product of the authors' imaginations or are used fictitiously. Any resemblance to actual persons, living or dead, events, or locales is entirely coincidental.

Cover art by Mark Jarrell

(https://markjarrellart.com/home.html)

The collection and arrangement © 2023 by Julian Barona.

Contents

* * *

Reviews

Introduction

Dear Reader,

The tyrant falls.

A familiar trope in fantasy fiction in general, and in sword-and-sorcery in particular. After all, Robert E. Howard's Conan ascends the throne of Aquilonia over the corpse of the tyrant Numidedes; Michael Moorcock's Elric slays his cousin, the usurper Yyrkoon, and goes on to struggle against the tyranny of the very gods; even Kane, Karl Edward Wagner's oft-villainous antihero, topples tyrants (even if the tyrant in question is himself). The popularity of this plot point is understandable. There is, after all, something eternal—mythic, even—about the tyrant's fall: the destruction of the old order, the righting of wrongs, the triumph of the eternal outsider against the cyclopean forces of the world, and so on. It is natural, perhaps, to imagine ourselves in opposition to the tyrannies of our own lives—which are manifold—and to seek in our fiction the victories that we may, or may not, achieve against those real-life oppressors.

But there is always the question: what occurs *after* the terrible king is overthrown? And is the tyrannicide themselves an inalienable hero by virtue of their one good act? Or might the aftermath, and its architect, be more complicated figures, bitter and sweet in equal measure?

This is, we assure you, not meant to rehabilitate the tyrant—let Numidedes fall, we say—but merely to examine the pleasant and beguiling complexities of a common, fruitful trope. Perhaps it is because of these pleasing complications that we find sword-and-sorcery so uniquely suited to depictions of the tyrant's fall. Sword-and-sorcery protagonists are most often outsiders—as Brian Murphy observes in his seminal critical work on the genre, *Flame and Crimson*—and outsiders sit squarely at the intersections of those many qualities that render a character multifaceted: admirable in one moment, and less so in the next.

Conan, for example, is a barbarian adrift among the civilizations of the Hyborian Age, a savage to the "civilized" peoples of the south, yet never quite at home among his fellow barbarians (notably, we never see him meet another fellow Cimmerian, or return to his homeland); civilization baffles and infuriates him, and yet, he always returns to it (and, of course, ascends eventually to the position of civilized ruler).

Elric is the hereditary emperor of his decadent, cruel people, but is estranged by his unique sense of morality and compassion, which even his dearest companions (such as his lover [and cousin] Cymoril) cannot quite understand; ultimately, of course, he destroys his own empire, scatters his people to the four winds, and becomes a wandering, sorrow-filled mercenary who, in the end, destroys his own world.

Kane is a man cursed by a mad god to wander eternally and live a life of shiftless, purposeless violence. He finds himself divorced from the common human experience by his omnipresent murderer's rage and, eventually, by the ennui of the immortal. And yet, for all his monstrosities, he often finds himself pitted against greater monsters than himself. Invariably, these vaster evils meet their end by Kane's red right hand.

There is then a complexity to the sword-and-sorcery outsider that defies straightforward heroic definition. Or rather, it recalls the heroism of the Greek, the Roman and the other pagan cultures of antiquity and the medieval era: consider Odysseus, who was strong and clever and yet (at times) a savage, deceitful and murderous man; consider Cú Chulainn, who was the greatest of all warriors and an impossibly beautiful man, but who slaughters his own son through his stubborn adherence to a hero's machismo (among other unworthy deeds); consider even Lancelot, who was the perfect knight and (one might argue) the perfect traitor, responsible for the sundering of Camelot and the deaths of everyone he loved, including his wife and his best friend. Such heroes are people of great virtues and equally great vices—gigantic mirths, and gigantic melancholies, one might say—and the good they create, if indeed they create any good at all, is often complicated by their other, darker deeds.

A compelling realism lies at the heart of this depiction of the hero. How often in our own lives have we seen the good mixed with the bad in some person's deeds? How often, when we glance back at the histories of our nations, do we see the same? How often, indeed, have we seen tyrants fall in our histories (or our presents), and rejoiced—and then winced, as some other evil (sometimes lesser, sometimes greater) afflicted us in said tyrant's place?

And yet, still we cherish our stories of the fallen tyrant. Perhaps all the moreso for their complexity. Maybe another quality of the sword-and-sorcery protagonist, as detailed by Murphy, can account for this: the sword-and-sorcery protagonist possesses, above all other qualities, an indomitable will. They see the odds stacked against them and swing a sword at it anyways. Death stares them down, and they hold its gaze without flinching. The tyrant is another form of death—the death of choice, one might say—and one which we all might encounter, even if only in the DMV line, or in our emails with a middle manager in the office. Thus, in defying death and the tyrant, the sword-and-sorcery protagonist does what we wish we could do: they strike back, and damn the consequences.

Not all of our stories in this issue of Old Moon Quarterly deal with tyrants and their downfall—but they all, to some extent, touch upon the outsider with the indomitable will. In our first story, "Pain Wins" by Sasha Brown, a Stone Age father wields his will (and a knapped stone axe) against the twin evils of sorcery and starvation. In e rathke's "Scourge of Gods," a lone swordswoman struggles against a mountainous god—or, perhaps, a titanic daemon. In Marion Koob's Shakspearean riff, "The

Witches were Mine All Along," a certain Lady plots—with an implacable ambition equal to that of any Kane or Conan—against her husband, who stands (for the moment) as usurper to the throne of Scotland. Kyle Miller's "Call of the Void" presents us with an unusual sword-and-sorcery protagonist: a somewhat cowardly cleric of an outer god who, as sole survivor of an eldritch massacre, must find some way to make amends and strike back against the murderers of his people. Jennifer R. Donohue's "This is Not the Only Kingdom" is perhaps the least traditional story of the issue, at least in terms of sword-and-sorcery: the aftermath of a portal fantasy, it deals with the grief and trauma that a child whisked off to a fantasy realm might feel in the aftermath of their return to our mundane world. Finally, we conclude with a weird, grim story of struggle and tragedy in Nelson Stanley's "Death to Your King, and All His Loyal Subjects," which, through prose penned in the tradition of Clark Ashton Smith, casts a weathered eye upon the notion of tyrants and their overthrow.

So read on, dear readers, read on! We hope you enjoy this issue as much as we enjoyed curating it.

Kindest regards,

The Editors at Old Moon

Pain Wins

By Sasha Brown

There was no meat. We huddled by the fire while the snow fell. All season we'd been looking for mammoths on the ice, but there were no mammoths left. Most of us fell and died. My mate, my child's mother, had fallen. Only a handful of us were left.

Now my child looked across the fire with anger in his eyes. "Why can't you find meat. I'm hungry."

It was painful to see him starving. I spread my hands. "I don't know. Maybe I'm not good enough."

Moss Teeth gnawed a stick. "There's no prey anywhere. It's not you. It's the world."

"Tomorrow we'll look again."

"Maybe we've come to the end of the world." Bad Face squinted into the flames. "No one here but us."

As if in answer, a shape came out of the snow towards us. We readied our spears and axes, but it was just an old man. He was thin and tall and strange looking, but still old, and alone in the blizzard.

"There's no food here for you or for us, old man."

Moss Teeth still held his axe. "We could eat him."

"Go. There's no room at this fire."

The old man took a handful of dust from a pouch. "I brought my own fire." He threw it over the flames, and they roared in our faces. We rolled away into the snow, howling, slapping embers from our ragged pelts.

We hunched together, afraid. The old man wore the shaggy ochre skin of an animal I'd never seen. He hunched over a gnarled stick with a strange skull affixed at the top, and pointed across the fire. "I have no child. I have been through the world and found power you could not imagine, but I have no child. I will take this one."

"This one is mine."

"Nevertheless, I will take him."

From another pouch he drew a different dust and blew it out, thicker and hotter than fire smoke. We choked and cried, writhing in the dirty snow. It blinded us; it made us claw at our throats; it puffed out our flesh in red panic. It felt like crawling fire.

I couldn't find my child but I could hear him. "Father, help. Why don't you help me?"

By the time we could see again, the old man was gone.

He took my son. The fire was out.

I stood with my axe. "I'll go and get him. You stay here. Start the fire."

Bad Face shook his head. "That's a sorcerer. Bear Tribe met one. He was tall and skinny and he killed a lot of them with magic. You can't fight him. He'll eat you."

"Those are just tricks. I won't let him eat anybody. I couldn't save his mother but I want to keep my child. I can't make any more."

I took my axe and set off through the snow after the sorcerer.

The blowing storm filled in his tracks and I lost the trail. I was still looking when the sun went up, and still looking when it came down again. I looked for a long time before I saw the spark of firelight deep in a cave up the mountain.

I crept up and hid by the entrance, axe ready, squatting in the filthy snow. I couldn't hear anything. I thought he was deep in the cave. I waited until my breath was calm, and then went in quietly.

There were loose stones all around. I stumbled on a pebble; a larger one came after it, and another and another, until a boulder rolled down on top of me. I tried to jump clear but it caught my ankle, splintering it under the rock.

Then the sorcerer crept out of the shadows. My child was in the corner behind him, wrapped in one of his ochre pelts. I pulled but my foot was crushed under the boulder. The old man was a coward but he was smart. He'd set a trap for me. I was stronger and I thought I could kill him if I could hit him with my axe, but he kept out of reach. I was a dog in a snare. He could kill me slow, from a safe distance. My child would watch me die and know I was too weak to get him back.

The old man had a long tube and he slipped a dart into it. "You shouldn't have followed. You see, boy? My magic is too powerful for him."

I was caught like a dog, but I knew what dogs did when they were caught. I'd seen it, and if an animal could do it then so could I. I had something to teach them both still. The old man raised his blow tube and I readied my weapon. "No magic. A trick. A trap. A balancing act with rocks. Clever but not magic. I have a trick for you."

I chopped my axe into my leg. The pain made me scream, but it split my shin from my ankle in a few strokes, and I left my foot behind. Blood spurted from the stump. I dragged myself up and leaped towards the old man, but he shrank away and ran deeper into the cave.

My child watched me. I hopped to the fire. "See. Magic doesn't win a fight. Pain wins a fight."

I drew out a half-burned log. "If it's an animal, then it's just who is faster and sharper. It's instinct. But people know about sadness and pain. We have to think about it. Whoever is willing to hurt more, that's who wins."

I pressed the burning end of the log into my severed ankle. I screamed again, but the fire stopped the blood.

The boy shrank back, staring at the smoking blackened stump of my leg. "How will you hunt mammoths now."

"Wait here. I'll go and find this old man and kill him."

"He knows real magic."

"I'll be careful."

I lurched into the dark. The passage grew narrower and I couldn't see anymore. I heard a puffing sound, and a dart stuck into my stomach. It burned when it hit and the burning spread quickly. I felt it inside me, green and rancid, and it made me stumble. I fell out into a wider cavern.

A blade rattled against the stones just where I'd been, clattering up the passage behind. It wasn't the heavy clunk of a stone blade. It sounded sharper and meaner. It sounded like ice breaking.

It was dark. It stank in this cave; it smelled rotten. I held my breath and heard the old man panting in the dark. I raised myself to my knees, listening to his breathing and cocking my axe. I threw it, grunting and falling with the effort. But it was a good throw and it thunked into flesh.

The old man shrieked and I dragged myself after the sound. I felt blood under my hands and followed it until I touched his foot. Then I crawled up his skinny body and covered him. I could see just enough to make out fear in his eyes. He reached for his pouches and I batted his hands away, slapping them up, trapping them between us in front of his face. Blood made it slippery between our bodies, and I could feel my axe. It was in his chest. It was a bad cut, but not deadly.

"You're no sorcerer." The poison was still seething in my veins, but it wouldn't kill me. "You're cheating. These are tricks. You're just an old man. I've come for my child."

The old man spat blood into my face. "It's all real. It's all magic. You're not the only one who knows pain. Pain is stupid. It just makes you hurt. You want to see magic. Watch." He grasped his smallest finger and wrenched it down and it cracked and broke, and at the same time I felt the bones of my forearm snap inside me.

We both gasped with pain. My wrist hung like a split stick. "What did you do. What is this trick."

"It's magic. I've worked so hard to learn it all. I deserve someone to teach it to. Look at you, starving and wretched in the cold. You should thank me for taking him away."

"He's mine. He's the only thing I have."

The old man held a trembling hand in front of my face. He took another finger in his fist. "Selfish. Watch, I'll do it again." He bent it back, crying out as it broke. My other arm fractured and went crooked.

I couldn't move much, but I had weapons left. I fell down on him, gnawing at his face with my teeth. He screamed and struggled but I found his eye and sucked and chewed until it popped in my mouth, and that made him lose focus. I tried for his other eye but he cringed away and I found his cheek instead. I bit through it until my teeth clicked against his. Pain wins a fight. I would gnaw through his face to his brain.

I yanked back, feeling his meat tear. He screamed and whimpered. My mouth was full of blood. My child had crept in behind us. I recognized his breathing. I spit the old man's flesh out. "See, child. You fight until someone shrinks in horror. It's whoever's willing to hurt more. No tricks left now, old man."

"Look at you." Some of the old man's lips were gone. "You're an animal." His one eye gleamed in his mangled face, looking over my shoulder. "I have one trick left."

The dagger bit into my back. It went in and out many times, that mean weapon. Sharper and more heartless than my stone-carved axe.

I rolled over, choking and staring at my child with the bloody knife in his hand, and I heard the old man's voice in my ear. "Your child is mine now. It's my best trick yet." Then everything was pain and blackness.

I only woke up for a short time after that. I didn't know how long I'd been in darkness. A fire had been built; on the other side of it was the boy, eating. The smell of meat filled the cave. The old man was propped against the rocks, watching me with his one good eye. His chest was bandaged, and his jaw was showing where I'd bitten his cheek away.

The boy stopped eating and looked at me. "He's going to teach me magic. He'll show me how to do it."

"He's a coward." Something had collapsed inside me and I was having trouble breathing.

"I won't have to be hungry and cold anymore. You couldn't even stop my mother from dying on the ice."

I tried to rise but my arms were gone, and I saw my hand on the other side of the fire, in the boy's grip. The meat was sucked from two of the fingers already. Finally then, I shrank back in horror. It was too much pain for me.

The boy dropped his food and crawled towards me, his cold blade in his hand. My lips split when I moved them. "Don't. This old man is full of tricks. It's cheating."

"No. It's magic."

Scourge of Gods

By e rathke

She sheathed her sword in the scabbard on her back and dug her bleeding fingers into the grooves of its scales. Pulling herself up, she gasped at the stab of pain in her bruised and fractured ribs. The scales felt rough against her calloused and torn flesh but she climbed, digging her toes into the spaces between scales. Blood flowed from the beast like a river, but its body still breathed. She climbed a mountain of flesh, the surface rapidly expanding and contracting.

She panted along with its great body as she climbed higher and higher into the thin mountain air. The sun was bright and hot but threatened by rushing clouds. The wind ripped at her tattered cloak and battered straw hat, both fastened round her neck. She dug her fingers and toes in, held her breath while pressing herself tight against the warm body of her kill. Blood dried beneath and inside her nostrils. Every breath was agony.

Standing on the beast's great chest, she limped towards its head, across a landscape of undulating flesh, hard scales and soft feathers. Sputtering lungs and a hammering heart beneath her feet rattled her body. Staring down at its enormous snout, at the jaws that could hold her body a dozen times over, she swallowed hard and exhaled loud. Her body swelled against the tears and cuts and bruised bones. Her steps came light and her head flooded with images of what would greet her at the mountain's base.

"Human." Its breath burst hot from its panting jaws, its voice deep as the roots of the mountain.

"I'm here, monster," she said, her voice like tempered iron.

It laughed. Losing her footing, she groped for balance in the shifting, dying body. She pulled her sword from its scabbard, the black metal scorched by the great beast's blood. Gripped in one hand, her other hand spread wide for balance, the sword's weight caused her shoulder to scream in hot weariness.

"Human." Its voice crashed like thunder against her ears. "Why have you come?"

"To kill the mountain monster."

Laughter came like an earthquake, convulsing the giant body. She tumbled and rolled to her feet while stabbing her sword into its chest. The laughter transformed into a howl. "You foul little monster!" the beast's voice shattered. "I dreamt of this day and of you, caustic pest! You once shouted my name in joy and worshiped me as your god! You once sent your priests to me as sacrifice! How long has it been? The moon lies to me from this high."

Using the sword as an anchor, she stood again. "The gods don't die."

It snorted. "Say my name."

"We don't name monsters."

Laughter rolled from deep in its deflating chest but only came as a long drawn exhale. "It's been so long. You've all forgotten. Forgotten who you were. Your dawn was my twilight and the sun's been setting for so long. So very long. Even the mountains only crumble now. I hear it. Its bones creaking, cracking, and turning to dust, tumbling down to the earth below."

Her brow furrowed as the beast spoke, its long jaws clacking and its tongues fluttering to make human speech. Dozens of eyes stared up at her while dozens more stared off into the sky, to the mountains near and far. Huge bloodied tusks protruded from both sides of its jaws. The horns caught the sunlight and flashed in rainbowed colors. The wind ripped over its enormous body, dragging against her tiny human form and the blood-heavy clothes she wore. Lightning blinked far away and thunder clapped against the darkening sky as the sound of distant rain crashed.

"Tell me," she said.

The beast's heart slowed beneath her feet and its lungs filled with its own blood. Its voice wet and thick, it said: "They called me Oklololompo. Hundreds of your short lives must have passed under that name. Then I was only Lompo for a hundred more. Now you tell me I am nameless. Only a nightmare for the descendants of those who worshiped me for so long." It coughed and spat blood. "Tell me, human. Tell me your name."

"Vinshya."

19

"What does that mean?"

Vinshya pulled her cloak and straw hat tight against the blustering wind. "It's only a name."

Oklololompo snorted and gobs of blood flew into the air. "You have all forgotten."

The rain came in sheets, battering against Oklololompo's flesh like a thousand drumming mallets. Vinshya pulled her hat lower and sat on Oklololompo's chest, hands still clutching her sword hilt.

"Human," Oklololompo shouted against the storm. "Kill me, if that's your task."

Vinshya counted Oklololompo's breaths as the storm raged past them.

"Human, are you still there? I see nothing but the dark."

"Say my name," Vinshya shouted.

"Vininsiya," Oklololompo said through gasps.

"Close."

"What joy is there in watching me die?"

The rain ran in rivulets from her straw hat. Her eyes closed, she focused on her breathing.

"Tell me, Vininsiyaya. Tell me what they say of me."

The cracking lightning was the only response.

"Please, cruel killer. My life is yours. Only tell me. Or kill me. End this pain. I have never known such pain as this. Not only my body. But death. I see the darkness crowding my vision and I want to run. Flee. Escape. Escape this darkness. This pain in my soul."

As quickly as it came, the storm drove past them, leaving them wet and cold, the stink of decay already thickening the thin air. Flies swarmed towards Oklololompo's severed limbs strewn across the plateau.

"Human?"

"They have forgotten you, monster."

Oklololompo whimpered and convulsed. "You are cruel. What have I done to deserve cruelty from my killer? Is it not enough that you watch as I rot? My death-reek is so strong it's solid between my teeth. Its taste clogs my throat."

The flies buzzed, the wind moaned, Oklololompo whimpered, and the sun peeked through the blanket of clouds. Vinshya stood and pulled her sword free of Oklololompo's flesh. Blood oozed from the wound and clung to the black blade. She flicked her wrist, a slash through the air, sending the blood from the blade.

Now clean but for the scorch of the blood, she gripped the hot blade with her free hand. "You will die and I will watch you until your hearts and blood no longer live."

"Coward."

"To kill a god is to curse oneself."

Oklololompo laughed raggedly. "I thought I was only a monster."

"All gods are monsters."

"What will you do with my body, Vinshya?"

Vinshya cocked her head to one side. "I lied to you before. My name is not Vinshya but it's what I'm known by. It was given to me by people very far from here. Across the mountains and the ocean. My name is Laioa. Its meaning doesn't matter but it is beautiful. Like you, the name given me is who I have become."

"Before I was Oklololompo I was still me."

"But you were a different you, just as Laioa is not Vinshya."

Oklololompo's gasps were wet and bubbling in its chest. "Humans." It snorted. "Word games."

Vinshya said, "You're no longer Oklololompo or Lompo. You're the monster of the mountains. The demon of winter. The nightmare of mountain children."

Vinshya covered her mouth and nose with her cloak to block the pungent stench of death. The flies buzzed and the wind calmed.

Oklololompo sneezed a spray of blood into the air. "Tell me something beautiful, human. Let me know beauty before I die."

"No."

"Cruel. So tiny but so cruel. I will die with only the memory of your sting and the severity of your words. The horror of your eyes watching me bleed. Is that why you remain?"

Vinshya sheathed her black sword. "They say the gods see the future in their final moments. That those who hear them will see where their road ends."

Oklololompo's voice came weak, "I see nothing but the darkness. I have no future to give you. I would curse you but I can't seem to care. You are cruel and small and your curse is to be human. No, there is only darkness. Everywhere. Death."

Vinshya jumped down to Oklololompo's neck. Her feet sunk into the soft flesh until they struck the spine. Oklololompo made a clicking noise and choked under her weight. Standing in the shadow of its immense skull, she stroked the underside of its jaw. The soft feathers, and those matted together by blood.

"You were beautiful, Oklololompo. Goodbye. I am the scourge of gods and none will know your story." Vinshya's words dripped from her lips as a whisper.

Oklololompo exhaled long and blood flowed from its ears.

Vinshya jumped down to the rocky plateau and limped to its ear. The canal was wide enough for her to climb inside. She stepped in and spoke the meaning of her name.

The sun began its descent beneath the spines of the mountains and she made camp in the shadow of Oklololompo's dead body. She used its feathers as kindling and ate one of its cheeks as a feast. The powerful stench of its rotting body and the swarms of flies filled her dreams. Her dreams were of darkness. Of a road leading nowhere, lined by the dead.

In the morning she made her way down the mountain to collect her reward.

The Witches were Mine All Along

By Marion Koob

Macbeth, her husband, is just where she wants him: standing on the south-west rampart of the castle, sword brandished, raving nonsense at the moors and the forest stretching out beneath.

She is just where she wants to be: several paces behind, staring out at the same view. Undulating hills of gray-brown, and in the distance, the jagged lines of pines. Her expression is even. Macbeth has not seen her yet. When he, at last, turns and catches sight of her, his beloved wife—she re-arranges her face. She is good at it, tugging one end of her lips down, widening her eyes, twisting her hands round and round each other. She exhales a soft, eerie moan.

He flinches.

Her dress is torn. With great care, she made the gashes herself, in her chambers with the help of her Gentlewoman. The Gentlewoman held the skirts while she stabbed them, running through the wool with a dagger in long, measured strokes. For a moment, the two women caught each other's eyes, and allowed themselves a small smile.

Almost there.

On the rampart, she lets out another, louder, cry. Her husband—once Thane of Thamis, once Thane of Cawdor, now King of Scotland—her husband, gullible man, shouts for the doctor.

"You must make her forget," Macbeth orders, when the healer arrives. He goes on to say much more, but no one is paying attention. King Macbeth is tediously dramatic, she thinks. No simple sentence will do when a lyricism can be concocted.

"Pluck the ill from her mind," he is saying now, and calling for his armor, and swearing that he will never be defeated, for woods do not walk.

Soon, he will see that they can. He will see how Birnam Forest can be persuaded to come to Dunsinane. If, that is, she can trust Macduff to deliver.

He was stunned at first, the ever-earnest lord Macduff, to hear of her plans. Yes, she told him, her voice at a suitable quaver. Yes, Macbeth had indeed murdered Duncan; and Macbeth was, in the privacy of their chambers, already spiraling into madness. She had gained by his evil deeds, she had become Queen, but she worried for her realm. Was it not her duty to remove a usurper?

They'd carved out their schemes, quick, in the castle stables of Inverness, before Macduff had run for his life. If he was surprised by her detail, her specificity, he showed no sign of it. It would be the work of a few months, a few months at most, she said, and natural order would be restored to the kingdom.

Macduff, of course, was only ever a small part of her design. She likes to imagine the moment (soon now, so soon) when her husband understands her treachery. "Why—why," he'll choke, lying on the floor, bleeding out from the kiss of his rival's blade. She'll lean in and whisper, so that he knows, he knows how long she has been preparing. She'll lean in, and say: "The witches. The witches were mine all along."

She had hired the women, slipped coins in their palms, furnished them with the words that would move her husband. They'd returned triumphant with mud-laced locks and ashes sallowing their skin: "My lady, he believed it all."

From there on, simple work for the lady to coax, to encourage—to underline the opportunity of the King's visit.

Then, simpler still; pretending to madness, to grief; all to rile up guilt. Slipping the herbs in his drink, whispering *Banquo* until the ghost appeared; and, at last, the deal struck with Macduff.

Every step towards his downfall. Her husband's, and Duncan's.

"Why?" King Macbeth will say, coughing out blood, the red seeping into the flagstones of their courtyard.

Why, she thinks, can't a lady be ambitious? Bored? Can't a lady wish to evade hollow years on the moors, and draughty stone halls devoid of laughter and companionship? Devoid of nothing but the comings and goings of her husband and his horde?

Can't a lady wish to avenge? Avenge parents and cousins, murdered on the orders of Duncan?

A lady, she'll say, a lady can wish for these things and more. A lady can kill better than any man, quietly and feel not a mark on her hands. Her fingers now, as she stands on the rampart, in the wind, by the doctor, her fingers are pale and cold and clean. They look dainty, elegant. She looks forward to placing them in the hand of a lord asking her to dance. Macduff, perhaps? He has, after all, become recently unattached.

At last. They have broken through the castle doors. From below, she hears a crash, and clangs of metal and grunts of exertion. Meanwhile, King Macbeth has understood the trick of the forest, and is screaming his misfortune. He rants now about never meeting defeat from a man born of a woman; another deceptive truth she has planted in his ear.

It seems safer to retreat, and the healer is too distracted to stop her. She walks behind the crenulations to the door in the tower. There is a comfortable room there with a window from which she can watch, high up above the central courtyard. Macduff's men will know not to harm her. In fact, she hears the very man's voice now, gruff from fighting, shouting her husband's name. It will be over soon.

Heavy steps, ringing against the wooden staircase. She shuffles her skirts, runs fingers through her hair. She finds her most pleasing smile. Macduff will make a suitable new husband; an indisputable favorite of the next King.

He wrenches open the door, and she stands, turning toward him. His eyes are wild and ruthless, so ruthless that she is not, perhaps, as surprised as she should be when he grabs her arms, and instead of embracing her—lifts, lifts, with extraordinary strength, lifts her up and out.

Through the window.

Call of the Void

By Kyle Miller

In the end, his erratic bowels saved his life, for he was in the privy when the Haunted Knives swept through the outdoor theater and killed everyone they could find. Cahmül was the only one they couldn't, and he waited silently, his ass burning and leaking blood into the vault, his left hand resting on the silver moth at his breast. Its wings caught the narrow moonlight beaming through a hole in the roof of the privy where someone had plucked (like an eye) a knot from the wood. *When still, you merge with the quality of darkness. When active, you are on the same wave as light*, he prayed, holding his breath against the slightest noise, listening for footsteps and waiting for the shrieking to end, the anguish of battle made sonorous by the acoustics of the Celadon Theater. It was dawn before he could breathe freely and leave the privy to learn what he had hoped and feared: that he, and he alone, had been spared. He would have to pay the Survivor's Tax; already, the shackle of putrid mushrooms was growing around his left ankle. Spores fell from the mushrooms' pink gills and drifted through the air, reaching the membranes of his nose and mouth. They tasted metallic, like the face of a coin. As the chemicals seeped into his bloodstream, he became melancholy and weepy. A small mouth opened on the largest mushroom and said, "How could you?" in a voice only he could hear.

Cahmül despaired. What could a humble priest of Moth of the Void do to halt the evil perpetuated by the Haunted Knives in their mad and unknowable quest? He had only petty orisons and a light mace in the shape of a moth's body, more religious implement than weapon. And his intemperate guts—they had thwarted him on the battlefield before. There was nothing more wretched than doubling over with cramps and the stinging shits as good men died around you because you couldn't reach them in time with your small blessings of medicine. Using his belt knife, he shaved off a few of the mushrooms growing on his ankle, but it was painful to do so, and they grew back in seconds. Vengeance was the only release. Cahmül did not have the strength.

"Do more by moving slowly," he said, wondering if the old proverb might become true only by uttering it often enough aloud so the stars might hear it. He would start here, and continue one step at a time. Start here, by consecrating his sister's body against further evil and abuse.

A patrol from the Unking's Army marched into the theater as Cahmül searched for his sister's body. They took him unaware; he was distracted, half-blind with tears from the Survivor's Tax. He should have been more alert. The patrol would be seeking information about the slaughter, assessing future threats as well as collecting treasure: a gilded cup dropped mid-drink as the reveler threw himself in front of his daughter or a constellation of hand-polished garnets almost indistinguishable among drops of a jeweler's blood. They said the Unking slept on a hoard of such things, his tail wrapped tightly around the screaming Scepter of Agony and Avarice. His soldiers were said to be ghasts and soulless ghosts who fed on carrion and despair, but for all Cahmül knew, that was just superstition and midden-talk.

But when the captain pulled up beside him on his catoplice, one mailed hand resting on the beast's sweaty neck, Cahmül reconsidered. He smelled like a dead mongoose wedged in a flue and all that could be seen of his body beyond its brain-like armor was the bottom half of a pale, goatish face.

"You've guilt's mark," the captain said, his voice clear and startingly human. He might have been any stranger met along the road with that voice.

"I need to get to the Academy," Cahmül said. "I need help. Tell the Unking that the Knives endanger the balance of the realm."

The captain kicked Cahmül in the face, and he fell backward into the void.

* * *

When he woke, the air wore rain like a gray gown. His hemorrhoids felt like cinders pressed against the tender flesh of his anus, and he cried out, but there was no one but Moth to hear him. And Moth, in his way, was silent. After a futile trip to the

31

privy, he found his sister's body, diced to pieces by the Haunted Knives' magic blades. It was said they forged their knives from tear ducts harvested from the witch Antipole's grass puppets. When the puppets had achieved the sentience they asked for, they had then asked for the gift of emotion, and the Witch delivered. The puppets shed tears of joy and madness, but soon discovered regret. They felt sorrow and hatred when the Knives cut out their ducts to forge their blades. Magic made the knives invisible and incorporeal; the paradox lay in their ability to wound regardless. Some said even a scratch was enough to leave one weeping for days, inconsolable, beyond the comfort of mothers and grandmothers. The Haunted Knives, inhuman and unfeeling, their true nature hidden perhaps even to themselves, needn't worry about an accidental cut, though they rarely made mistakes. Cahmül could not defeat them himself, not as he was. He needed to call upon a higher power, one not so distant as Moth: his master, his mentor, the Professor of Dust and Ashes.

"I'm sorry, sister," Cahmül said. She was the reason they had come to the theater. She wanted so badly to see the *Rotten Magician's Song*. She had seen less than half of it; the Knives had arrived during the second act. "Leisure was the end of you, as father once promised it would be. Moth buries you in his wings." He lay what remained of her in a pit dug with a stage prop shovel, said a prayer to protect her soul against desecration, and left, unable to look at the slaughter any longer.

Step by step, he thought, like Eadginu King of the Void, who walked blindly through the greasy black curtains of Nighthome, step by step, guided only by his faith in nothingness. *Follow the ten blind steps of Eadginu.* He thought of his training, navigating a bed of coals while blinded by spellwork. He thought of the burns. "Take the second step," he said, thinking of the man who trained him, the master who forced him to walk the coals.

"What do they want?" the shackle asked on the road to the Academy. An infant's unfinished face pushed through the skin of the mushroom cap and mocked his expression.

Cahmül gagged. "Who?"

"The Knives, shirker. Yellow-mouse." It reveled in offending him with the hundred names of The Coward.

"I don't know. No one does. They kill, but never steal, nor rape, nor leave anything behind."

"They answer to a greater will then?"

"Like you?"

"Perhaps I come from inside you. Run-rabbit. Deserter."

"Do you not want me to succeed?" Cahmül was losing his focus, allowing the Survivor's Tax to tear him apart from the inside. Why should he yet draw breath as the grubs of Saint Decay chewed on his sister's lungs? He felt that he wasn't being a very good priest of Moth of the Clear Mind, Moth of the Simple Heaven. His mind was a weak and easy prey. Run-rabbit, indeed.

"I don't care," the shackle said. "Perhaps I feed upon your failure, and success makes my death."

Cahmül thought he had never walked a longer journey. He was nearly strangled in the Swamp of Severed Hands, and on the road beyond, when he stopped to squat behind a giganteberry shrub to empty his guts, a missingfish crawled up his leg without his noticing. It almost reached the nearest orifice, his ass, with its necrotic tongue, seeking the soft tissues inside where it might make its parasitic nest for the next two months before ascending to reality, no longer missing, much to the chagrin of Cahmül's abdomen. But the shackle called Cahmül's attention away from the heavens toward the floor, and with a small prayer, Cahmül set the missingfish on fire. He refused the shackle any gratitude.

Cahmül wept when he saw Ringwhile Academy's wide and welcoming doors. He had learned very little in his time there, most of it spent shirking his studies and fucking his professor's daughter, and then his son. But near graduation, he had met the man who changed his life, the one who gave his soul to Moth. He owed him much. Cahmül made his way to the dormitories and found his mentor, the Professor of Dust and Ashes, sweeping the hall.

"*Those who seek it go afar and return again*," Cahmül quoted. "I call upon your help again."

The Professor was a swarthy man in an indigo cloak, silk wings embroidered along the collar. He swept the hall and gathered students' trash, set outside the doors of their rooms each morning. "I refuse."

"I need strength."

"Keep your voice down," the Professor said in a fierce whisper. His station was a disguise, his power so great he needed to disguise himself, lest those covetous of that power hound him until the end of days.

"I need strength," Cahmül repeated.

"Find it then. Pull it out of the void in your heart."

"Not like that. You know what I mean."

He stopped sweeping and looked at Cahmül's ankle. *"Those we name sages rest quietly in their places according to the hour and the minute,"* he quoted, a line from the holy folio of the Dyadagara, prophet of Moth. "You're not ready, boy."

"I don't care. Show me. Now." His bowels twitched; his tongue tasted like iron. He needed this. Seven years as a novice was enough. "I don't have the power to protect the ones I love."

"No one ever benefited from taking a shortcut to power. I refuse."

"Then forgive me." Cahmül prayed, and a paralytic silver jelly fell from the void and covered the Professor's spotted head. Although such a weak orison was ineffective against a master like him, he froze just long enough for Cahmül to pull the glove from his left hand and expose the Window on the back of it, a black square that acquired depth on closer inspection. It was like an impossible hole in his flesh, a window to another realm.

Cahmül defenestrated himself through the Professor's hand and fell into the void.

* * *

To face the void before one was prepared spelled absolute death; not death as a peasant knows it, but the death-of-deaths, your soul erased from the book of the world. You would wander as a milkwraith or join the Unking's Army and forget you ever had reverence for the thing called Creation. And Cahmül did love the world, or part of it, the part that contained the beauty of a sunrise on the Crepuscular Sea, or the glory of watching a doveknight earn his wings in an eruption of golden feathers. Perhaps he was among the last who revered the world. It was filled with cynics and nihilists, and many confused worship of the void with abject nihilism, but he was always telling anyone who listened how they were wrong, how it only made sense to worship creation from a place of nothingness because the void moves toward creation while creation itself can only move toward the void. People had trouble understanding.

Cahmül's hands tightened around the thunder of silence. He was suspended in unlight, in undark. His bowels churned and cramped. He was afraid of everything.

He called out to Moth, but there are no words in the void. You cannot call out to the void; the void can only call out to you.

Two enormous beaks appeared like the First Thoughts, pale blue and long as a crane's, and they picked him apart, tearing his wings off again and again, holding him prisoner of the void. He cried out to Moth in his weakness, though he wasn't in pain, only terror and loneliness, abandoned at the foot of the god's empty palace. *Caution on those who seek to meet their god*, he thought.

It's never soft clouds and warm delight.

"Moth! Do not forsake me, though I am but a scale upon your wings!"

And the void held him until he found the strength to proceed. At first, the waiting was intolerable, the outcome uncertain, and his mind tore itself apart: what else was there for it to do? But hadn't he waited in the dark of a privy for hours for something that might never occur? Endless hours wasted counting spiders and imagining new spells that would never be his to cast. He was good at waiting. He knew pain, tedium. He relaxed and counted the seconds.

By then, the world was much older than when he had left it. The void held him through a dozen massacres perpetrated by the Haunted Knives, held him until a new Unking slept beneath the tower and his sister's bones were eaten by an osteophage and the Professor of Dust and Ashes became dust himself, held him until he felt blossoming within his chest a valorous new will, a power capable of great good and great evil, and the peace of mind to wield it properly.

Cahmül's mind cleared. The beaks tucked themselves away and let his wings grow back. He saw—in the corner of his vision—the swift flutter of a pale blue wing like the page of an unwritten book curling in the moonlight. He dared not look harder. He let himself fall down and out, back into the world.

* * *

The Academy was gone, ruined by time and careless

stewardship, victim of an ideological war among its board members. Cahmül walked to the place he had last spoken to his mentor. It felt like a day or perhaps a year ago. It would be some time before he could adjust to living in the future.

"The hour is late," his shackle said. "You're running out of time, greentongue."

"No. I bloom late, like the century lotus in the deepest muck of the Conciliator's Waste. I make my own time."

The shackle shut up.

A tortured, wounded figure reached out from the jungle of weeds that had overtaken the ruins and scratched Cahmül with an invisible knife. He jumped back and felt a sudden sadness cutting into him, but he quickly banished it. He could clear his mind in an instant now. Such was the power he had received.

"Your mistake," he said, and he prayed a wreath of Void's Fire onto the Haunted Knife, pacifying its mind, turning its will toward Cahmül's own, toward a greater will, that of Moth of the Void.

"You'll tell me how you were wounded," Cahmül said, making a leash with his belt and preparing it for the Knife's thin neck. "And then you'll show me where you were born."

His bowels twitched, once, and went still.

A humble priest of Moth was helpless against the Knives, but Cahmül was no longer a humble priest. He was Cahmül, Son of the Void, and he would pay the Survivor's Tax if it took a lifetime. He would cleanse the world of the Haunted Knives' senseless oppression, and then he would find the wound that bled them into the realm and close it for good.

He began on that day.

This is Not the Only Kingdom

By Jennifer R. Donohue

I'm not supposed to remember. They told me I wouldn't remember, and at first I don't. I remembered only the frayed edges of this world, camping with my parents in Yosemite and then darkness for a time, a sense of weightlessness. Then days later, almost a week, almost a hundred miles away, rescuers found me near a cliff. They weren't even searching that area, they were going to refuel. But I remember the helicopter like a heartbeat, wind on my face, strong hands putting me on a bed, and then weightlessness again.

It's cruel, to know magic and have it taken away. It's cruel, to have a whole magical life and then be returned to a mundane world and a child's body. That's why I'm not supposed to remember. There are rules for this, older than anybody. Older than this world, which is younger than many of the rest, and the kind of thing that my parents wouldn't want me to say, ever.

By the time search and rescue found me, everybody assumed it wasn't a rescue operation anymore, but a recovery one. They tell me this later, of course, after I'm out of the hospital. After I stop speaking in a tongue they don't know and return to something more like the little girl that they thought they lost.

I understand that, I want to tell them. I lost my first husband, champion of the realm, when he went on a quest in the Maw Beneath the Mountain. It had not even been the first time he'd gone into the Maw, and he had the scar to prove it, a long livid line that ran the length of his back next to his spine, where he'd lost one of his beautiful wings. He'd gone the whole rest of his life unable to fly anymore, or even glide, wearing a heavy golden cloak that covered both his wing and his lack. I couldn't fly either, of course, and never minded his lack.

I can only assume the Maw wanted the other wing. We did not find his body, though I lassoed a gryphon with starshine and made the whole Court follow me out to the mountain. Either because I had nothing the Maw wanted, or because it was sated, the way to it was not open to me. I had to return home again alone, the entire kingdom in mourning for nine years.

But I can't say any of that to any grown ups, much less my parents. My mother, whose face grew sharp in that week, hollow-eyed, who grew nervy and seems smaller now, diminished.

"I'm okay," is what I say to my parents, my mother. From my hospital bed, dehydrated, tubes needled into the back of my hand and the crook of my elbow. It's the first thing I remember how to say right. "I'm okay." Things beeping and lights flickering and humming, making me think that my witch and confidante Serena is playing funny little pranks on me, but of course she isn't. She's the one who was supposed to make me forget, and I wonder if it's our closeness that damaged that spell, made it not work. Her name is the first one I lose, though I haven't yet. She kissed me for the last time as we stood there, and I put my hands in her hair one last time, and we looked into each other's eyes. "I don't want to forget," I said.

"I know," she said. One of her eyes twisted like a hurricane, blue and white, and the other one was entirely black, a stone from a magical serpent she'd killed deep in the earth. "And I will remember." It had to be enough. And we stepped apart, and I closed my eyes, and she began to chant. I was filled with dread and then lightness, and then there was the helicopter.

"I'm okay," I say, even as the sharpness of some of these memories are fading already, as I lose most of my adult faculties, and shrink down into childhood once again. I lose my queenly mantle and mien, but my posture never returns to anything like a modern, normal child in this world would have.

* * *

Back at school, we write our What We Did Last Summer essays, and as I fill the first pages of a notebook with my other life in the other world, I realize that I cannot possibly be honest. I lived a whole life during that week in the summer, or a life up until I saw my eldest daughter crowned queen, and then a curse fell upon the land that would only be alleviated by my sacrifice, the removal of my self from that realm back to the one from whence I came.

I tear up those pages, start over. I labor to relearn my clumsy handwriting with a scratchy pen, so different from the flowing script in shimmering ink that I've used all these years.

* * *

"I'm okay" is my real-world aegis, my spoken-word magic charm. For physical charms, I do what I can to approximate; my mother is pleased that I'm taking an interest again in the charm bracelet that she started when she was young and built up over the years. I've had my own since I was five, but only had a few charms on it that she got me, trying to make it a bonding exercise that I didn't previously connect with. Having had my own daughter and watched her grow to adulthood, I understand now. I reach out. I put the bracelet on soon after we come home, and I ask for a helicopter charm.

"I don't know if they make them, sweetie," my mother says, frowning. "But we can look."

"I'm sure they do," my father says, cautiously. He wants to support, but not interpose. I appreciate his tact. I notice it a lot now, of course, after spending decades at Court and speaking with diplomats. It's undoubtedly his example that allowed me to take to it as well as I did.

* * *

When my essay comes back with red pen all over it, I laugh, which my teacher interprets as poor behavior, but it isn't. Rather,

I'm delighted that I was able to mimic a child's poor language so well. It took me so much effort, and to be rewarded with a bad mark for it is very gratifying. I can't explain this, though, and laugh harder at how ridiculous it is, which sends my classmates into an unruly chaos, and sends me to the principal.

He reads my teacher's hastily scribbled note and looks at me appraisingly. I arrange my features in something like remorse. I've faced opponents, political and social, who were willing, and indeed tried, to kill me. I have no fear of this man.

"Why don't we have your mother come get you?" He asks after some deliberation. "It may be unfair that we're putting you through this so soon."

"Okay," I say, and sit in the office by the school secretary while he makes the call, and then I wait some more, and then my mother comes to get me.

"Don't say you're okay," she says without looking at me, once we're in the car.

"Okay," I say. If I could talk to her about what happened, I would tell her how much I missed her, and Dad. How it was exhilarating to be in a world with real magic, and there was hardly any time to think at first, but there were times, so many times, I missed her comfort. His strength. They're normal people, doing normal, small-family things: meatloaf and frozen green beans for dinner, evening news on TV, mowing the lawn on Saturday morning while I watched cartoons. I missed my parents, not the meatloaf. I burst into tears the first time I sat at the kitchen table, again, and it was meatloaf again. I'd just had a lifetime of magical feasts. Everything my heart could desire. Meatloaf and frozen green beans were such a terrible blow. Ketchup glaze. Glass of milk, always the glass of milk. They didn't even have *cows* in the other world.

"Can we get a charm for my bracelet?"

She looks at the clock in the dashboard, and sighs. "Yes."

I'm thinking of a quill, which they might not have, but a feather would do, or a pencil. The store is at the mall, and we park by the movie theater, and I look at the movie titles as we walk past, but I don't know what anything is. How do kids find out what movies are? Television, I guess.

I notice the man watching me before my mother does, and I hide my notice, to see what he'll do. He lets us pass, and then says, "Ma'am, excuse me? Excuse me, I'm sorry to bother you, but can I speak to you for a moment?"

She hesitates, turns. She does not want to speak to him. "What is it?"

"I was just noticing your daughter's posture, and I was wondering if you had ever considered a career for her in modeling? I can give you my card, I'm an agent for —"

My mother does not have my father's diplomatic polish, or that week of worry wore it away, and she steps too close to him like a fencing master going for a finishing strike. "Get away from us," she says with a crack in her voice. "I know what you people do to children and it's disgusting. I don't ever want to see your face again, get away before I call the police."

He's shocked, utterly, and I just barely keep from laughing, tears filling my eyes from the effort. "Jesus, lady, I didn't do anything. I was trying to give you an opportunity to—"

"I'm not telling you again," she says, striding forward more and he's backing away with his hands up, his business card fluttering to the floor like a flag of surrender.

He retreats, shaking his head, and doesn't look back. My mother waits for him to be out of sight, then sits on the nearest bench in a sudden slump. I recognize the relief of a battle deferred, or perhaps won, and I hug her. She's shaking. "Mom, it's okay."

"I'm supposed to tell you that," she says, giving me a squeeze and then pulling back to look at my face. "I don't know what came over me."

Having killed at least one man over the safety of my daughter, I know. I know, and I can't tell her. I don't miss the feel of steel on my hips, constantly, the only thing I was able to learn in order to defend myself reasonably, as I had no wings and learned only the slightest of magics. My starlight and gryphon trick couldn't fix everything. I don't miss the way a blade feels once it's connected with living flesh, bitten beneath the surface, nicked against bone, released blood in a hot shower. I'm happy to have survived, and am so aware of what I paid, even if sometimes now it's in fits and starts, just splashes of memories, impressions.

"You were protecting me," I say, almost too late, after the moment is almost gone.

She pulls out a tissue and wipes my face; apparently I was still crying. "I will always protect you," she says, and a shadow crosses her face. "However I can."

"I know, Mom." We always want our children to be safe, and well, and happy.

* * *

I'm having a sleepover for my fourteenth birthday when a raven knocks at the window. The other girls titter and shriek and say that it's a branch or a ghost or a murderer, but when you've spent a portion of your life ruling in towers and receiving messages by bird, there's no way to ever mistake the sound of beak against glass.

It is impossible for this raven to be here. It is impossible for me to ignore it.

I take a lacrosse stick and say that I'm going to bravely defend us all, and go outside. I forget to pretend that I need a flashlight. I've amassed enough charms on my bracelet, and remembered enough of the tiniest scrap of a ritual and tried it again and again enough times that I got the barest echo of it to work, and can see in the dark when I want to. Most of the time. This is one of those times, or it's a full moon and doesn't matter.

I got my first period, again, and started to grow boobs, again, and tried out for the lacrosse team. That was new, that was different, there is no lacrosse in the other world, and it seemed

47

like a good way to still be able to take a field of battle in this one, that wasn't too close to anything else. My own thing, different from my other life.

The raven is not one I recognize, but that shouldn't be a surprise. The surprise is that there's a raven at all, and I look at him skeptically. "Why are you here?" I ask, and then wonder if we'll even have the means to converse.

He hops closer and cocks his head and says, "Your daughter has died. The queen is dead, long live the queen."

"What? She died? What *happened*?" But the passage of time is so different, between there and here. How could she have even still been alive? I won't ever know. I shouldn't know.

He watches me with his inkblot eyes, darkness in the darkness. "She was very old, and very loved, and one of your grandchildren already took over the throne several years back. She wanted you to know. She has always mourned your loss. We all have."

I'm crying, of course. There's no shame in it. I didn't think they would have still held me in much regard. "It worked, then. Me leaving saved the land."

"It did, your majesty. We are daily grateful."

"I'm so glad," I say. "Tell them—" and then the door behind me slides open and my friends chorus,

"Elowen, what are you *doing,* did you *die*?"

I startle and look back at them. "I'll be right there! It was just the wind, it knocked a branch off the tree that I'm getting out of the way."

"Hurry up!"

"*Okay.*" I sigh, turn to take my leave of the raven, but he's gone. A feather remains in the dewy grass, and I pick it up gently and stroke the smooth edge. I should have asked his name.

Without thinking, I press it against the inside of my arm, and there's a small blue flash and the feather sinks into my skin. I stop and stare at it for a moment, a long black tattoo on my pale skin. How will I explain this to *anybody*? I can't. There's no explanation.

I go inside and lean up the lacrosse stick. "There, I protected you all from the big mean wind, aren't you grateful? And on my birthday!"

"You're so brave, Elowen!" Maria, the goalie, holds out two DVDs. "Here, pick which one, we're going retro tonight."

"Ooh, retro." I take them, wait to hear a 'what's that?' or notice anybody's head turn, but nobody notices my feather. Maybe they can't see it. Maybe it's just for me. The movies are *Labyrinth* and *Pan's Labyrinth*, and I laugh. "These aren't related, you know."

"That's the joke!" Maria says. I pick *Pan's Labyrinth*.

* * *

I'm a rarity, the sporty nerd, because in addition to lacrosse, I read nearly every fantasy novel I can get my hands on, the portal fantasies included. I'd almost rather not, because they make me yearn for something I cannot have. The Pevensies returning to Narnia, Quentin Coldwater becoming a king of Fillory, Alice refinding Wonderland, Dorothy continuing her adventures in Oz. It isn't fair. It was also my duty, and I was an adult when I made the decision. I'm very lucky, to have lived an entire life of magic and adventure, and now I get to live another life, one of relative safety, with things like electricity and flush toilets and the absence of evil wizard curses.

I don't feel lucky, I feel melancholy. Unfulfilled. Lacking. I try, I try so hard, and I see my parents trying too. In some ways, I think they're still in Yosemite, searching for me with growing panic, sure that I am gone, I am dead, and they will never see me again or even find the body. That they found me not quite the same was, I think, always explained to them by professionals as trauma; whatever has changed about me was my trauma response to whatever happened to me in that survival situation.

My dad sold or threw away or burned the camping equipment after that, though. I never saw it again in the house, never stumbled upon it in storage, never saw the slightest remnant in the attic or basement or garage. All of our clothes for camping, down to our boots and water shoes, the tent, the coolers, all of it. We were a stay-at-home family, a stay-in-hotels family, after Yosemite. A never-go-anywhere-alone-ever family, a call-me-if-you-need-a-ride-I-don't-care-where-you-are-or-what-y ou're-doing family. He used to be so outdoorsy and adventuresome. He took up woodworking instead.

I try hard, I try *very* hard, to honor my parents in the real world, and obey their rules, and not worry them further. I did not want to be a 'troubled child.' I was a grown up too, once. I was a *queen*. I understand obligations and responsibilities. Obligations and responsibilities, and my honoring of them, are what robbed me of that life I had built, that place that boring real-world me had carved out in that magical land, and I resent this, sometimes. I rankle at the limitations and, I'm sorry to say, I act out. Not as much when I'm still an actual child; ironically, I'm able to control myself better than, make myself smaller then. But when I'm a teenager, when I'm in high school, and I have to have what at first is a calmly requested conversation about getting my driver's license and then a screaming, tearful, door-slamming, foot-stomping dragout fight, there is a shift. No, they don't want me to get my license. Why would I need my license, when they can always drive me? Where do I need to go, that they can't take me?

When I start to get mail from colleges and when scouts from teams start calling my coach, my mother nervously says, "well, why don't you stay local for the first year, just to see how you cope?"

I don't even say anything to her. I enter such a blinding, white-hot fury that I turn on my heel and walk out of the house, and down the street, and a block later, girls from school recognize me and pick me up and take me to a party at a lake house that somebody's parents own.

I always thought that movies were lying, and nobody in high school was actually having parties like that. They were; I just wasn't invited to them, until I was. And when I was, I saw a different world, full of shifting allegiances and with hedonism as the goal, and this is an angle I never considered: doing what I want, simply for the sake of it.

* * *

My grades slip a little. Not a huge amount, not enough that I get in trouble. I've forgotten more, recently, and it upsets me, agitates me, in a way that I of course can't explain to anybody. I can only act out like a teen. And even so, I don't act out all that much. My adult self would be mortified at such behavior, even as my parents here would be, and I cannot betray myself, and them, so far as that. I sneak out to parties. I drink at parties, I smoke some pot. I drop acid, *once*, and it makes me miss the other world so hard that I sob until I throw up.

I still make practice and play hard and coaches keep calling my coach, and my coach keeps calling my parents. And I keep shaving off the margins of sleep, of staying home, of toeing that obedient good girl line. I slip out of the house, the window if I have to, my insomniac father asleep on the couch in front of infomercials, and I run to where somebody will pick me up. I wear my varsity jacket to do it, ironically or defiantly, or as a kind of armor in this different hierarchical world. I drink and I dance and play the stupid party games, and comfort crying or throwing up girls in the bathroom or in the bushes, and there's a time of night, when the lights are smeared at the edges of things, that I kiss somebody.

Of course I kissed people in my other life. Kissed people and more; I had a daughter, with my first husband. I did not, with my second husband, and then not with my…well she wasn't my wife, but I'm not sure if consort is the correct word. I've forgotten the language, by now. If I ever really knew it; I might have always only spoken English, and they all understood me anyway because of magic. But I waited a long time to kiss anybody, like this, in the real world. Again, I did not want to trouble my parents. I did not want to be a problematic child, or an alarming one, and I absolutely never wanted to have another baby again actually. Not here in the real world, without magic. Painkillers were not the same thing.

I kiss boys, and I kiss girls, and I think the girls appreciate it more. I've got more experience in caring than most of the boys they've made out with do, and I wonder more than once if it's wrong of me to mess around with anybody that I'm going to school with, because I was an adult once. But I was never an adult *here* and that's why I don't stop. Anybody I kiss wants to kiss me. Anybody I take my clothes off with wants to, furtively in the backs of cars and in bedrooms and one time in the locker room of a rival team at an away game, and that wasn't nearly enough time to get everything done, but we returned to the field with more energy in the second half of the game, if with some shake in our legs at first.

* * *

I go to college. Away, not community college. The fight for that is days, weeks. Months. My mother resolute, my father supporting her, both of them saying that they only want to protect me. They only want what's best for me. Me saying that yes, they did that. They spent years doing that, they've done such a good job, we all made it. And now it's time to open up more. Not stop protecting me, I could never ask that of them, but let me fly, and fall, if falling is what I do. Let me come home if I need it.

"You can always come home, sweetie," my mother says, and doesn't understand my immediate sobs. I can never go home, I can't even say. Everybody I've known will be dead by now. My name will only be a legend. There's only so long a populace can be grateful, I do not begrudge them. But I *ache* for what I had and what I lost, and there's no solace for it.

I think my episode of tears is what convinces them, somehow. That I'm not doing this out of petulance, or to hurt them. That they're suffocating me. That I don't want to leave and forget them, I just want to live my life. My second mortal life.

College is only a couple of hours away, and it would be easier if I had my license, and that's something I'll work on next summer. We pile together in the car, the trunk packed full of my stuff, and drive away from our town, take a highway, then wind on little back roads that make me feel like we're going camping again, but of course we never went camping again.

They don't put on the radio the whole time we drive, my father's hands too tight on the steering wheel, my mother trying to make tearful, fragile conversation. I have a credit card for emergencies, and a bank card linked to an account I didn't even know I had. It's not like I've ever been allowed to get a job.

I know how they must feel, I remind myself. They're overreacting, I think, but it's how I felt when I told my daughter goodbye, before the witch and I went to the standing stones where she would perform the ritual to send me back and make me forget. I've never been able to figure out why I didn't forget; I haven't the tools here, and no witches or dryads or anybody to ask. I've only ever seen one raven. This is a difficult goodbye, from my parents who thought they lost me forever once. They don't want anything to happen while I am at college and they are at home, and they have to just remember the inadequate things they did or didn't say before they drove away after leaving me at the dorm. Every goodbye, to them, has felt like forever. Every morning. Every night.

I need to tell them where I went, I think, again and again, with increasing urgency, every time we pass a sign that says how many miles left to my college town. They need to understand that there's nothing they could have done. There's nothing I could have done. There was a prophecy, there was a ritual, and I was plucked from this world and into the other. There were tasks that they needed fulfilled, that only a benign, powerless human could complete. They need to know that they didn't fail me by losing me for that time. I'd gone someplace more wondrous than any of their imaginings. I'd had a whole *life*—

"Elowen?" My mother, turned around, brows knit. This must be at least try number three to get my attention.

"Sorry, I was just daydreaming, what's up?"

"You were so far away," she says, and from the flinch around her eyes, I know she hurt herself saying that. "I was asking if you wanted to stop for lunch or anything?"

"Why don't we go to lunch in town after we get there?" my father asks. From his tone, this also isn't the first time he's said it.

"I like that idea, I think," I say. "That way I'll have someplace here where I can go when I want to think of you."

My mother reaches out and grasps my hand, and my bracelet rattles. "You can call us whenever you want," she says.

"I know."

"You don't have to do this," she says, and I can almost hear my dad thinking about the deposit.

"I'm okay," I say, and she flinches again, all of our old hurts resurfacing. But we need to do this. It's important that we do this. I have a growing certainty about it, like when I approached those standing stones for the last time, felt their hum in my head and chest and throat even if I couldn't hear it, not exactly.

My father parks in front of my dorm, where a student in a volunteer shirt points us. I'm not the only one moving in today, of course. While my parents wait anxiously at the car, I approach a girl with a clipboard. "I'm Elowen March," I say. "I need to sign in, I guess?"

The girl runs the back of her pen down the page, finds my name, turns it around to check me off. "Here you are!" she says, and she smiles brightly at me, one eye blue and one eye brown. She picks up a manilla envelope from the plastic tub next to her, and it rattles with keys and is fat with paper. Her name tag says Serena. "We've been waiting for you."

I blink at her. Serena. Still smiling, she looks at my charm bracelet. She looks at my tattoo, actually *looks* at it. I smile back, slowly, cautiously, a tickle in my memories, which have already been so close today.

"I'm so glad," I say, taking the envelope, still standing there a moment longer. "I need to—"

"I know," she says. "But we'll be seeing a lot of each other, Elowen March."

"I hope so." I look at her over my shoulder one last time as I get back to the car, and when my mother grabs my wrist, it startles me. "Mom what—"

"Elowen, what *is* this?" she asks, and apparently she can see the feather now too, after all these years. I've dreaded it for so long that I forgot instead.

We all look at it together; it isn't completely plain black, it's got a deeper sheen to it, mostly blue, but some purplish and maybe green, like an oil slick. My fingers tingle, with a memory of magic that I have not felt in some time, of that moment before you take a breath to speak words into the world that will change it forever, of that moment before stepping into the possibilities of the unknown.

Death to Your King, and All His Loyal Subjects

By Nelson Stanley

On the far side of the mountains there was nothing—a desolate shore studded with outcrops of black rock, a dark and churning sea.

Guizer, a tall man, scarred yet still upright, had freed us from those who'd chain us to their oars or to their fields. He roused us now, exhausted as we were by our wandering, and we scrabbled along the foreshore for what could be gleaned: a strange crab-like creature here; a rubbery plant there, crawling upwards in a cleft between black rocks; the little driftwood that studded the gray sand under the caliginous sky.

Flames here were slow to kindle. A few bits of salted wood caught, and over their meager warmth we roasted the crab-things and the rubbery plants. As the day waned, a sudden storm sprang up, killing our fires. We huddled together under sodden cloaks.

Perhaps the fading light fell just right against the crags or some trick of the gloaming prismed the breakers' spray, but just offshore we saw the dark shape of the island, a shadow-place where before there had been nothing but rain and open water.

There came a tall figure from out the heart of the storm, walking ashore from the sea. The waves lashed about its shoulders and ebon spume gathered about it like a mantle or a cloak. Its mien was difficult to discern: edges penumbral, shifting ribbons of soft darkness that trailed behind it and dissipated into the violent spray; its center umbral, a bottomless, starless void. It stalked across the surface of the sea the way a man crosses a rutted field—with care and determination, but with no more difficulty than that.

There was no animal upon this shore save the deformed crab-things, but behind the figure came a flock of carrion birds, heavy of wing and cruel of beak. By guile and subtle movements they hung in the sky despite the storm, apace with their master, two lines flung out diagonally behind it.

Guizer hefted his war-axe, held it up as if to salute us, then strode down the beach to meet the figure as it emerged from the waves. It was as if darkness had become embodied in the rough figure of a man, a tenebrous giant that towered over our chief. Children cried; men trembled; women muttered wards. The great carrion birds settled upon the sands, eyes a-glimmer in the dying light, their patience and silence as terrifying as their master.

"Hail," called out Guizer. "We are a free people and make all welcome. Sit down by our fires and share our meager repast."

The tall figure spoke in a sonorous voice, a voice drawn up from depths:

"Your fires are extinguished."

Guizer laughed.

"You are observant, friend. Tell us, who are you who walks in from the sea?"

"I am the King of Shadows," it said, as if this should suffice. "I know of you, Guizer, and know of your people. I know of your plight and of your journey. I come to make an offer."

The carrion birds cocked their heads to one side, as if they could understand the words being said, looking from the dark figure to our chief and back again.

"We welcome friends wherever we find them," said our leader. "Sit with us as we discuss your offer, so that the people may have their voice on your assay."

The wind blew harder and tendrils of darkness trailed from this Shadow King and wisped into the gloam. Guizer held the thing's blank gaze, then cut his eyes quickly to the sword hanging at its side, a black broadsword plain and unornamented.

"I think not," said the Shadow King.

The figure gestured whence it had come. In the failing light, the apparition of the strange island had faded, its outline now indistinct through the mizzle.

"The way closes. The time is nigh. Come with me and live out a life beyond the reach of those who drove you before them, or dwindle your last upon this blasted littoral."

"Such decisions must be taken in common," said Guizer, and those who had known him long noted the way he shifted the grip on his axe, the subtle rearrangement of his posture.

"There is no time," said the Shadow King. "Follow me now, or be forever lost."

The arc of Guizer's swing was flat and true, with no tell in the stroke; the bit clove the air with enough force to sunder an armored man and his mount besides. This King of Shadows reached up in the languid manner a man dozing flaps at a fly and caught the haft just below the blade. Then it reached out its other hand and touched Guizer upon the chest and Guizer's face took on a terrible livid cast and, without a noise, he fell upon the sand.

The Shadow King—and was there, now, the suggestion of a terrible crown upon its head?—dropped the axe on Guizer's corse. The carrion birds shifted but made no effort to settle about the body of our leader.

"I come not to do battle, nor to debate," said the Shadow King. "Simply choose. Those who would live, forever beyond the reach of your foes, come with me now. All who stay here will be lost."

And this Shadow King turned and strode out into the sea, and as he strode forth all saw that he walked into the arms of the waves not as men might—that is, struggling through surf and reaching for the solid bottom as it slips away beneath their feet—but rather upon the surface of the waves themselves, as one struggles through weeds on solid ground. We looked out at the dimming isle; we looked back at the mountains whence we had come, blacker than the gathering night.

As one, the tribe lurched to feet frostbitten and mutilated and followed this Shadow King across the pounding surf to its tenebrous island.

I cannot tell you how the waters bore up under their weight, but the people followed the Shadow King and not one fell by the wayside. Gradually, the rain slackened, then stopped; when the air cleared, there was no island upon the dark sea.

I alone stayed upon the sand. I did not trust this King of Shadows. I sat and I sang this song to the rocks and the mountains and the sand and the pounding breakers and the strange crab-things and to the corse of our leader and to all that gathers in the dark, and I wondered whether I should ever see my tribe again.

When she dropped from the darkening sky, my heart stopped within my chest; it was only when she uncoiled her great bulk of a tail upon the sand that it set going again, with a thump that I felt throughout my bones.

"Little man," she said, towering over me. "Little singer. I can see you have been done a wrong."

She smelled like the sea: marine and mineral and old. She had no arms but great pinions, hinged on one wicked claw, composed of a membrane like a bat; they fluttered ragged to their edges with a noise like wet washing smacking upon a line. Instead of hair she had a coxcomb of quills arcing back from her brow, a spiked mane down across her shoulders and back. Her breasts were naked, her skin dark, but it was not her nakedness I stared at—at least, not that portion of her nakedness that resembled a human being. Her serpentine tail was thicker than my waist but her voice was sweet and human, and it might only have been that which stopped me from running into the dusk.

"Little man," she said, and the great wyrm of her lower body uncoiled and slithered so that she might level her face with mine. "From my perch on the rocks above, I saw your leader fall. We have a common enemy, for I have seen you weep your desolation upon this shore. I too have wept in my time, and known desolation, and the Shadow King has been its cause."

My thoughts were blinded by terror. I fumbled for Guizer's axe. She leaned down closer, so that I might smell the sulfur of her breath, and I let the weapon go.

"Wise decision," she said, and there was humor in her voice. Her great compound eyes glittered, and a million stars gleamed back at me from their depths. "If you took up such a weapon against the Shadow King, you'd end up as dead as your leader, little man." She smiled, terrible and predatory in the moonlight. Her teeth were fishhooks, all barbed in her maw, and a forked tongue slicked amidst them. "But I can show you a weapon that would strike fear into the heart of the Shadow King, were he to possess such a thing as a heart. I can show you a weapon that would tear his form asunder."

At this, at last, I found my voice.

"I am no warrior, m'lady. I sing of battle, not take part in it."

She shook her head, rattling her quills.

"With this weapon, a child could strike him down."

"If that were so, m'lady," I said, "would you not have employed it against our mutual foe?"

Her tail beat a great tattoo upon the sand, in time with the breakers upon the shore. But she smiled again and said in that same pleasant, even tone of voice:

"You are clever, little man. I would fain take the weapon and strike that crown from his head, and his head from his neck along with it. Alas," she said, unfurling her great ragged wings so that they blotted out the darkening sky. "Alas, my form is not conducive to the wielding of hand weapons, and my bulk"—her great wyrm-tail lashed and coiled—"prevents me from accessing the place where it resides. I need your help, little man." She closed her wings and settled down so her eyes were level with my own.

"I offer not the twisted bargain of the Shadow King, for my sense of justice is acute. If you will not aid me, climb upon my back and I will speed you to wherever you wish to go, if it be within my power. Otherwise, I will show you where the weapon lies, and I will show you a way to the land of the Shadow King. The choice is yours."

"The Shadow King offered us a choice," I said, disbelieving that I managed the words even as they came out of my mouth.

"True," she said, "yet I do not threaten to leave you to die, as he did. So what will it be, little man?"

I looked up at her, impossible and mad and strangely beautiful, her quills shining blackly in the moonlight so I knew not if they were bone or metal or something else entire. I looked down at Guizer's corpse.

"If you'll tell me your name, m'lady, I'll be the instrument of your revenge."

"Call me Kelaino," she said.

* * *

I clung to her spines and her quills, knees straddling her thick torso. She smelled like apothecary's things, things that scour the inside of the nose and smart the eyes. Her hide was slick, thick and bluish, cool to the touch; when I looked behind me I realized her tail was mottled like an eel. Beyond that, do not ask me any further, for I clung on for my very life as the wind of her passage threatened to send me spiraling down to the ground far below.

She must have flown for a very long time, for I fell asleep astride her, lying along her great back. When I awoke, dawn threaded the horizon. She wheeled about, lowering, gyring toward our destination.

I screamed.

The cliff-face rushed towards us. We skirred towards a ragged rock wall whose jagged tops loomed hundreds of feet above the black waves.

She looked over her shoulder, and the dawn caught the facets of her eyes.

"Hold on tight, little man," she said, her voice coming through the buffet and the roar like a knife. "Or our scheme will have ended afore it's begun."

She dropped one wing and rolled lazily, a falcon cutting the escape of a thrush, and headed for a great jagged split in the rock, maybe twenty feet across, stretching from the pounding surf nearly to the top of the cliff.

We entered and the world and the wind dropped away into sudden darkness. Then, we were out the other side into the light, and she rolled back level and beat her wings hard, fighting to gain height. Below us, the sea surged through the chasm in the rock into a vast bowl or crater about which the waves crashed with a noise like thunder. Spindrift pattered down upon us like the finest rain.

"I've reconsidered," I gabbled, leaning close to ensure she heard me very clearly. "On second thought, Guizer was a tyrant and I never liked him anyway—"

She laughed cold and mournful and pulled up, flying vertically, a demonic arrow shot from the center of the world. I left my stomach behind; one more second and I would have lost my grip but then we righted and she touched down upon the top of the cauldron.

"Here, little man."

A few yards in from the cliff edge there was a mound of earth, maybe seventy feet across and twenty high. Looking closer, one could see that the lower edges of it were rife with large bluish stones, piled together to form a rough circular wall before the soil was moved back over them. I walked a little way around it, trying to stretch the feeling back in my legs.

"What is this?"

"An ancient grave. The warrior within was interred with his weapon, and it is his weapon you must retrieve to revenge ourselves upon the Shadow King."

I backed away, legs unsteady again.

"Look there," she said, and pointed with the claw upon her pinion to what I, at first, took to be a mere cleft in the mound-side.

I realized that three of the larger stones formed a sort of small doorway or lintel, though the entrance was half-choked with soil and fallen stones, and the gap thus framed looked to be so low that I would have to get on my knees to squeeze into it. I looked from the entrance to Kelaino.

"Our people revere the dead."

She laughed her bitter laugh.

"Then we are lost, for we will not stand against the Shadow King without the weapon within."

I stared at the horizon, then back at the grave-mound.

"I'll do it," I said, taking my first step toward the barrow. "But if I'm going in there, I'll need a torch to light my way."

She laughed again.

"You may depend that you do not, little man." The inscrutable facets of her eyes flashed like obsidian. "Just one thing: touch nothing but the weapon within. Time may have forgotten the horrors that were interred since this grave marker was raised, but the occupants of this mound have not."

I had to contort myself, putting my head nearly across my hip before I could wriggle into the narrow gap. Soil pattered down upon me as I eased into the damp stone and wet earth, but Kelaino had spoken true. Once thus insinuated, I found if I wormed in—more from the motion of my shoulders and spine than my limbs—I could make progress through the narrow channel. The bluish stones were cold; the freezing soil fell into my mouth and gritted my eyes; a chill had my bones. I pushed myself further, contracting and contorting—by some prodigious working of my neck and shoulders, gaining purchase mostly by, I think, means of my chin— until it seemed I had turned a corner in the narrow passage and then, suddenly, the rock I was braced against was no longer there. I fell downwards.

I opened my eyes in darkness. There came a scant ghostly light from above. I moved my aching body, checking to see if I had suffered any great injury from my fall, then I turned my head and screamed.

I had been alone in the dark, with only the faint suggestion of outlines to stop me braining myself on any jutting stones or outcrops of rock. Then I turned and the cave I found myself in was lit as if by a billion tiny points of green fire, weak and fitful as a candle that gutters and threatens to fail.

The grotto was bedecked with vast stone columns and strange, urn-shaped protrusions, half-wrought, half-grown in the viridian twilight. Water dappled from the vaulted ceiling. All was jagged ridges, tortured folds, prodigious shelves of fretted rock wet and a-glisten like flesh, whorled and jagged. Off to one end, the cave dwindled into a black hole with the suggestion of a rough channel leading upwards into darkness.

I landed in a circle perhaps ten feet wide, marked out by stones such as had been used to build the walls of the barrow above. Within this circle—as well as myself, some few moldering bones and a grinning skull wrapped about with frayed cloth—lay a sword. Its hilt shone, and it was festooned with what seemed like precious stones, though in the green half-light they all looked like emeralds.

The pile of bone shivered, then rose, trailing its cerements, skeletal arms open in a ghastly embrace. Its touch was icy. Shattered ribs and jagged bits of shoulder jabbed my flank. Its teeth clacked inches from my ear. We rolled amidst the remains of its grave, bodies bucking like two lovers tumbling over and over upon the rocky ground.

Its breath—for somehow it breathed!—was hot dust; the rags that I at first thought held it together tore like paper. I tried to throw it off me—managed to get one knee up between us to pry it free—but I overbalanced and fell again to the floor. Its teeth came together again, closer to my ear; by its soft halting exhalation, I realized it was trying to speak. It was not clawing at me but rather climbing up me, the better to reach my ear.

A sudden wrench of pity went through me—tempered perhaps with disgust at my own fear. I ceased my struggle and lifted this thing of rags and bone near to my ear.

Its whisper tickled the cusp of hearing like the sound of dust shifting in empty rooms, susurration more than speech. I lifted it and felt the faint stir of its fading breath in my ear, mausoleum halitus.

"All's lost..."

I threw the thing from me. It struck the wall and this time came to pieces, the skull shattering, vertebrae rattling into crevices, all animating force spent. I groped about for the sword.

The gold quillons blistered and blackened, twisting away like ash in the wind. As I touched it, the jewels melted from their sockets and dripped and ran away upon the cavern floor, the gaping holes left behind withering and seeming to pucker as the surrounding metal blackened and flaked to the ground. The bright blade dulled, notches and chips appearing along its edge. Within seconds it looked like one could do more damage using it as a club rather than trying to cut or thrust. One of the cross-guards fell off with a sad, dull clink.

What remained seemed less a weapon than a suggestion of one, a vague sword-shaped implement, all that remained after aeons in the ground. I wondered if its remains were worth returning to Kelaino when I looked down and saw something shining wetly from my side, as if the green light of that place had turned to liquid and stained me.

I drew back my furs and saw that one of the dead thing's broken limbs had dug into my side; a mere scrape across the flank, though it bled freely enough. I rearranged my clothes over it, even as I felt the merest stirring of something inside the wound, a not unpleasant prickle.

I wrapped the sword in the tattered cobweb of the winding sheet and bound it to me as a makeshift scabbard, then made across the cavern floor into the black hole, the floor of which indeed sloped upwards. Soon, I turned a corner and the soft green glow faded. There in the absolute blackness, I began to see strange things, to feel strange things; even though I am sure I climbed higher at every step, a great pressure seemed to build in my brain, as if all the mantle of the planet bore down upon the meat within my skull.

Small pinpricks of light jumped and flickered like bats' wings at twilight. I lost my sense of the limits of my body, drowning in darkness and dissolved in the abyss; I seemed to both expand infinitely and collapse under the immense weight even as, at a far distance, my feet thudded upwards and the rough, cold rock of the passage wall scraped my hand. My ribs itched and ached. Something uncoiled there beneath the world, a huge movement in the far blackness, a thick churning that started in illimitable depths. I became one with its writhing, both part of its fluctuations, and as if I were flexing a part of myself.

Voices came to me, at first as soft as the whisper of the skeleton, then a growing clamor: children crying, hawkers in bazaars, screams of warriors bleeding their last under alien skies, ancient dirges of priests in echoing lost cathedrals, rousing songs around a tavern or campfire, voices thundering and pleading, the tumult of royal proclamations from high towers, the sanctified calls of a thousand unknown faiths leading worshippers to pray; the baying of crowds, near-silent half-sobs of the broken-hearted in lonely rooms, lovers' whispers as they died into each other and shrieks of torment echoing back from hot metal and grim torturer's stares, children playing and crying and the soft, companionable noises old men make when resting in shade with their fellows: distant sobbing, carefree laughter, tortured screams.

Then, still blundering along the wall, I felt the cold kiss of a sea breeze, smelled salt in my nostrils. I emerged blinking into the light, in a cave-mouth which, when I poked my head out of it, I realized was set a few feet down from the edge of the cauldron upon which the barrow stood.

Kelaino must have known where I would emerge, for as my eyes adjusted to the light her thick tail slipped around me and hoisted me into the air. She set me on the ground before her.

"Tell me, m'lady," I said, "do you not fear that I might test this weapon upon yourself?"

Her compound eyes were blank.

"I do not believe you'd be so discourteous, little man," she said, her voice honey and guile, "but even if you were, how then would you get to the realm of the Shadow King?"

"This is true."

"And of course," Kelaino said, smiling her terrible fishhook smile, "we have a bargain, little man."

I smiled back.

"That we do, m'lady. That we do."

"One thing, little man. The former possessor of that blade. He didn't touch you, by any chance?"

The wound on my side throbbed and pulled as if at the behest of some strange tide. When I blinked, strange and terrible sights came to me, of things I remembered not, the weight of thousands of years upon me. Behind my eyes, empires rose and fell; wars sputtered to their ignominious ends; figures who were not quite men toiled to drag cyclopean blocks of stone across a desolate plateau for the glory of unknown gods; trusted viziers stepped from the shadows to knife me from behind their smiles, again and again; friends—battle-comrades, sisters-in-arms—withered and died from age or treachery or violence. Something insinuated its way through me, root and branch, creeping along all the venous and arterial pathways of my body, through the warp and weft of me.

"He was aeons dead ere I found him."

She gave the merest nod and offered her broad back for me. As we beat into the sky, I looked down the ragged coastline, through the spray. Disappearing off into the distance, set along the tops of the cliff until cut off at either side by the mountains my tribe had crossed, a succession of burial mounds stood watch out to sea like bonfires set to guide a fleet home.

* * *

A storm rose on the horizon and Kelaino turned toward it, skimming over the breakers. Lightning flashed in the heart of the squall. Kelaino put back her wings and we descended through a mad rush of air, the louring horizon a mass of fractured, roseate light. Down we plummeted through the raging salt air and she skimmed the crest of the foaming waves, trailing a spilth of water as she banked and before us—where a second before there was only the ever-churning sea—was the Shadow Isle, the desolate realm of the Shadow King.

She landed upon a low and lonely promontory of blackened stone, a spit of rock thrust out over the pounding surf.

"Alight here, little man. I cannot go nearer. Go now and strike true, for both of us."

She writhed her great serpentine bulk about and deposited me upon the glassy rock, uncoiling her tail so that she leapt, hanging for a second above the roaring waves before flapping heavily upwards, beating down the wind. I watched her ascend until the speck of her was lost.

I made my way inland through the rain. The island was formed of the same hard, glassy rock as the promontory, and I saw neither soil nor water but for the spray and the rain.

The heat and pulse from my side rose to a pitch. I was the only living thing on that weird isle; not a mouse scurried nor a beetle crawled. Onwards I wandered, heading always away from where Kelaino had deposited me. Soon I saw a rocky outcrop covered with a great congerie of shabby forms, clustered over and squabbling amongst clefts and shelves in the rock; as I closed with them, I realized that this great profusion of shuffling, hunched figures disporting in silence were the Shadow King's carrion birds.

There were far more of them than I had seen upon the shore when their master took Guizer's life, and the great mass of them chased each other or pecked at their fellows with their great curved beaks, all of them sullenly seeking shelter from the blast of the storm; but not a sound did they make apart from the scrape of their talons on the rocks.

I thought that they might raise an alarm, take wing and fly to their master, but though some eyed me as I passed, the main ignored me.

A little further on I found him, sitting immobile on a throne that might have been carved from the black rock or might have been eroded that way by the pitiless wind. He did not stir at my approach; he sat hunched and maybe a little forlorn, his blank, dark countenance staring into empty space. I drew the ancient sword and approached, an uneasy sense of familiarity shadowing each step.

He didn't even move as the blade passed through him. His head tumbled through space, trailing darkness like smoke; by the time it rolled to a halt at the base of his throne, only a crown of bone remained, ancient and yellowed, crazed across its surface with a myriad of fine cracks. I watched his body fall in on itself, prodded disconsolately at the shrinking puddle of darkness which, within a few seconds, dissolved into the air. I turned to the carrion birds, but if they'd noticed the assassination of their master—or cared—then they gave no indication of it, and remained silently brooding or bickering as before.

Across the sky, illumined by violet flashes of lightning, streaked a black comet. It descended like an arrow, a thunderbolt, a curse from the gods.

She struck me with such force it should have broken every bone in my body, should have left me a puddle upon the faceted rock. The force knocked me perhaps a hundred yards, ricocheting off outcrops, bouncing off boulders. By the time she'd reached where I'd tumbled to a halt, I was pulling myself to my feet, finding. with the last dying ember of my surprise, that I'd even managed to keep hold of the sword.

She came at me again, low across the black rocks, a scream parting her lips, tail a-lashing, wings spread wide as doom, great talons unsheathed from her fingertips, riding the howling wind out of the heart of the storm.

I smiled and hacked off her wings, first. She shrieked high and wordless, a noise to stop a mortal heart. Stepping around gouts of black blood, I grasped her coiling tail and beat her against the rock face until she stopped squirming.

The light was dimming in her eyes. She coughed up more tarry blood, clots and lumps of it catching on the barbs in her maw.

"You lied," she managed, and I shrugged and ran her through with the sword I'd used on the Shadow King. As her carcass fell, I noticed that the sword seemed remade, now a plain black broadsword and—blurring away from the edges of my flesh like black ink spilled in water—tenebral filaments fluttered from me before they disappeared into the wind.

I shrugged and went to retrieve my crown from the foot of my throne.

Reviews

Son of the Morning
by Mark Alder

Reviewed by Graham Thomas Wilcox

Mark Alder's *Son of the Morning* begins on familiar ground for historical fiction fans: it is the mid-fourteenth century, and war between England and France brews. However, soon the story diverges from the well-worn pathways of our real-world history and ventures down a stranger path.

We meet the kings first (or close to first): Phillip of France, and Edward of England. Both seek God's favor. Phillip (called the Lucky) seeks to mollify Jegudiel, his patron angel, with beautiful art and grand cathedrals, in hopes the angel will accompany his army to war. Edward, the third king of England to bear that name, knows (for reasons that become increasingly clear over the course of the novel) that he cannot coax his angels from their chapels. In alliance with his mother (and noted sorceress) Isabella, he seeks other, more infernal, aid. Beneath all the struggles of these kings and their knights, other figures lurk: Osbert, conman and pardoner, who finds himself an unwitting tool in the fight for Hell; Dowzabel, a Cornish boy raised among the Luciferians, who worships the Morningstar as a figure of tyrannicidal liberation; and others, including Orsino the mercenary, Bardi the usurer, Edwin the daemonologist, and others, up to and including Jegudiel and Sariel, both angels of the God, as well as Satan, chief gaoler of Hell, and Lucifer, chief inmate of Hell (and lord *in absentia* of Free Hell).

The story that unfolds from these characters traverses the length and breadth of fourteenth century England, France and (of course) Hell. Much blood flows, and much weirdness ensues. *Son of the Morning* is, all in all, a rollicking romp of a novel (an impressive feat, given its 700-some pages), and one that—for all its breakneck pace—manages to penetrate towards some rather intriguing themes around the nature of political autonomy, divine right, and even the virtues of courtly love (or, perhaps, courtly lust). There are some cons to balance out all these pros, but all in all, I found *Son of the Morning* to be an enjoyable, if somewhat flawed, historical fantasy story.

Son of the Morning debuted in 2014, published by Gollancz and written by Mark Alder, the *nom de plume* of Mark Barrowcliffe, who also has written fantasy under the pseudonym M.D. Lachlan. For the rest of the review, I'll keep calling him Mark Alder for the sake of continuity. I was a big fan of Alder's Viking Age historical fantasy, which began with the (somewhat inauspiciously titled) novel *Wolfsangel*, and continued with *Fenrir, Lord of Slaughter* and *Valkyrie's Song*. In them, you can see a lot of the blueprint for *Son of the Morning*: engagement with premodern ideas of religion and faith, a critique of the violence central to warrior aristocracies (and, perhaps, central to our own modern societies), and a healthy dose of complex plots, terse prose, and bloody action to wash it all down.

The high points of *Son of the Morning* come chiefly from two points: Alder's characterization, and his worldbuilding. Alder's characters, when they shine, are luminescent. Osbert the pardoner, Dowzabel the Luciferian and Montagu the knight were the three standouts for me: the last in particular felt like one of Alder's most rounded and intriguing characters. In many ways a dutiful knight and a devotee of chivalry, Montagu finds himself questioning his king and friend, Edward III of England, on more than one occasion. Once he meets Edward's mother, the beautiful and power-hungry sorceress Isabella, Montagu begins interrogating his own motives and actions. One gets the impression that Alder did not intend the reader to *like* Montagu much, but I found him perhaps the most human of the characters: flawed, yet capable. He would have made a fine sword-and-sorcery hero, in another life.

Dowzabel the Luciferian also intrigued me. He was in many ways the antithesis of Montagu: a peasant to Montagu's noble, a Luciferian to his Christian, a boy to his man, a character who becomes *more* in charge of his destiny as the story wears on, while Montagu finds himself increasingly enthralled to others. Interestingly, Alder uses both characters to investigate the social order of the medieval world he constructs throughout *Son of the Morning*: Montagu, like all of the noble-born characters in the novel, expresses extraordinary distaste for those lowerborn than themselves. They see their positions, and the hierarchy that supports them, as God's ordained reality—and, as we see in the novel itself, this is true (though not necessarily just).

Dowzabel, by contrast, feels explicitly representative of the commoner: born a peasant on the Cornish moors, he is a member of a minority religion (the aforementioned Luciferianism) which seems to be, more or less, modern political anarchism transposed onto a gnostic framework: hierarchy is evil, and the false god of our reality—Ithekter, as the Cornish name him (which means, if the internet has not lied to me, something like "The Horror")—has usurped the world from the communal, voluntary good and delivered it into the hands of the coercive, oppressive sociopolitical elite. Lucifer is the *true* god (it was he who manifested as the Christ, not Ithekter), and he awaits, imprisoned in Hell, for his release. Said jailbreak shall bring about the upheaval of the social order and a return to the paradise of common ownership and communal wellbeing.

Or so Dowzabel thinks. The reality, he finds, is a little bit more complicated. The poor and the downtrodden are not automatically endowed with virtue by their suffering (though the nobility do seem pretty much doomed to be jackasses from birth), and anarchy is not quite the utopia Dowzabel was told it would be.

This brings us to the second main strength of Alder's work: the worldbuilding. He paints a convincingly different version of medieval Europe, at times alien and at other times familiar. Alder is certainly writing about modern people with rather modern thoughts, for the most part—he does not quite achieve the verisimilitude of Gene Wolfe in the *Latro* trilogy, for example—but he colors it with enough of a medieval paintjob that it all feels rather convincing.

The religious aspects of the story were intriguing; Alder focused in the main on the alien nature of angels (who love beauty, and often dwell in the cathedrals erected for them by earthly kings), and the divide between the demons of Hell (the fallen angels of Lucifer's army, who fought for freedom against God) and the devils of Hell (God's gaolers). This tripartite division seemed a more interesting take on the usual Dungeons and Dragons-influenced hierarchies of Heaven/Hell one often sees in medieval fantasy. The strong class divisions of medieval society are used to good thematic effect by Alder as well, though of course, they more clearly mirror our own modern ideas of class than they do something genuinely medieval (which is not to say they are wholly ahistorical either).

Where the book fell short for me was, in a strange way, rooted in the same attributes that elevated it: characterization, and worldbuilding. While Montagu and Dowzabel are interesting, and conflicted, men of violence, and Osbert the pardoner is a very recognizable sort of picaresque conman (who nevertheless achieves some character growth throughout the story), many of the other characters, particularly the antagonists, fell flat for me. Charles of Navarre and his mother, Joan, seemed like cutboard cut-outs: vicious and power-hungry were their two defining traits, and they never really seemed to get any other quality appended to them. Isabella, Edward III's mother, was similar: she is played as the femme fatale sorceress to the hilt, and never quite deviates from that pattern. I think that a book like this can depend in large part on the quality of its antagonists: if protagonists, compelling as they are, never meet their match in equally compelling antagonists, I often find myself a bit bored, particularly when we see things from said villains' viewpoints.

The worldbuilding also faded for me as the novel progressed. Alder sets up some very intriguing thematic questions in the beginning of the novel, and touches upon some heady territory: the nature of freedom, the role of divinity, and so on. But he never quite ties them altogether. Indeed, as the novel progresses and we meet more of the supernatural denizens of the world—including angels, demons and devils—the initial weirdness of the world's presentation seeps away, and we're left with characters that are simply humorous extensions of humanity, albeit with a Boschian cast to their features.

Yet, despite some of these missteps, I felt *Son of the Morning* stuck its landing. The ending came together well, and I'm certainly willing to forgive a lot in return for a strong ending. I thoroughly enjoyed the novel, and for fans of medieval European historical fantasy, it's certainly worth checking out.

About the Authors

Sasha Brown is a Boston author with work in *Cossmass Infinities*, *Pithead Chapel* and *The Magazine of Fantasy and Science Fiction*. He can be found on twitter @dantonsix and online at sashabrownwriter.com.

Jennifer R. Donohue grew up at the Jersey Shore and now lives in central New York with her husband and their Doberman. Her work has appeared in *Apex Magazine, Escape Pod, Fusion Fragment*, and elsewhere. Her debut novel, *Exit Ghost,* is out now! She tweets @AuthorizedMusin.

Marion Koob is originally from France, but she has been living in England for almost fifteen years: in London, Cambridge, Liverpool and now rural Wiltshire. She is a freelance copywriter.

Kyle Miller can usually be found in Michigan's forests, turning over logs looking for life. He currently teaches first year writing at Eastern Michigan University. His writing has appeared in *Clarkesworld*, *ergot*, and *Three-Lobed Burning Eye*, and you can find more at www.kyle-e-miller.com.

e rathke writes about books and games at radicaledward.substack.com. A finalist for the 2022 Baen

Fantasy Adventure Award, he is the author of *Glossolalia*, *Howl*, and several other forthcoming novellas. His short fiction appears in *Queer Tales of Monumental Invention, Mysterion Magazine, Shoreline of Infinity*, and elsewhere.

Nelson Stanley lives and works in Bristol, UK. His stories have appeared in such venues as *The Dark, Vastarien, Kaleidotrope, Dark Void* and other places.

Made in the USA
Las Vegas, NV
05 March 2025

19074270R20052